Orc in Winter

Realms of Glister
Book One

Melisse Aires

Copyright

Copyright© Melisse Aires 2017

All rights Reserved

Originally started as a short story of the same title in the **Love Is ...Winter Romance Anthology, 2016**. This work has been expanded and revised.

Table of Contents

Acknowledgments..1

Newsletter 3

Blurb..5

Chapter 1..6

Chapter 2.. 18

Chapter 3.. 27

Chapter 4.. 33

Chapter 5.. 46

Chapter 6.. 56

Epilogue... 68

Terms and Places of Glister.. 71

About The Author... 73

Acknowledgments

COVER STOCK: CAN STOCK Photos, Deposit Photos
Cover artist : Melisse Aires
Editing:
Mary Hamm
Roxana, Freelance Books

Newsletter

Please sign up to get emails of new releases and sales.
http://sendfox.com/melisseaires

Blurb

MORWENNA, A WIDOW WITH an infant son, agrees to hide and nurse a poisoned Orc as a service to the Queen. The Orc was human as a boy, turned by a bite into an Orc Warrior. For her help, the Queen will give her an estate in the North, not far from Morwenna's childhood home.

As she gets to know Sherrow, she realizes he is a good man, not a monster. Sherrow heals enough to journey north before winter weather keeps them from traveling. The caravan they join is in the hands of rebels, and they must get away.

Sherrow has secrets — He is not as weak as he pretends, he has Orc magic, and he is in love with Morwenna.

Chapter 1

THE QUEEN LOOKED AT her healer and swept a gentle hand over the forehead of the Orc on the bed. "There are so few people we can trust," she said to Fiona. "The assassin is still out there, waiting to kill him. They have access to the palace, and despite all our efforts, we don't know who they are."

"We must move him. Even a drop of poison or any kind of violence would kill him. He is almost gone now," said Fiona.

"He is too young, and his life has had so many hardships," the Queen said. "Sherrow is like a brother to me, we are cousins who were raised together as children. He was forced to take the Orc bite when he was only twelve. I didn't hear from him for months. I thought he was dead. Even after that betrayal, he came back to the palace as my personal guard when we were teenagers." Tears ran down the queen's cheeks.

"The woman I have in mind is loyal to the king and still has a nursing babe. She lives half a day's march from the palace. We can get him there under cover of night, in an ordinary farm cart," Fiona said. "He will be much safer there."

Sherrow could hear them speak despite the constant ringing in his ears. Tadame was crying, he knew from the sound of her voice.

"Who is keeping you safe?" the Orc asked, voice barely above a whisper. His eyes remained closed. It was embarrassing that his normally deep voice came out in a weak, shaky whisper.

"Kordan and Palaver. They are loyal. Don't worry about me, Sherrow. You must go to this cottage, hide there. Recover." Queen

Tadame said. "It is the only possibility we have to combat the poisoning, or you will die. You will drink mother's milk until your stomach heals."

"I don't want to leave you." He opened his eyes. It was night, the only light came from the fireplace.

"You are the closest thing to a brother, to family, that I have here. I want you to live! Who else will remember Lindel with me? Who else played in the Wood of Halloran in the carefree summer days of our childhood? We are the only ones left who were children together. I don't want to lose you, too. We are afraid to bring a woman into the palace. She could be paid to harm you, or she herself could be in danger."

Her words were all true, Lindel, her older brother and his cousin, had disappeared twelve years ago and only the two of them still mourned him. Their childhood days ended then, and just a short year later he took the Orc bite and was changed into a monster.

"Don't want to leave you."

"I can ride there to visit you. When you are stronger, we will move you north. Maybe I can winter there with you."

Sherrow forced his eyes open. Tadame's tear-streaked face decided the decision for him.

"I will do it." He closed his eyes, exhausted.

Maybe I will survive.

MORWENNA SAT FOR SOME time in the firelight, rocking gently while her son slept, his mouth slack. He was such a beautiful baby with blond curls and long-lashed gray eyes like his father. Morwenna stroked his silky cheek. If only Bryce could have seen his son, but he had died weeks before Owen's birth. An arrow from a rebel archer had pierced his neck above the armor, and he had died in moments.

Bryce's service to the king kept them safe, even now. She had enough flour, cheese, and eggs, a garden full of harvest, a good roof, and firewood to keep the tiny cottage warm all winter. Life could be so much worse, especially for a widow with a small child. She rose and put the babe in his cradle near the fire, full of straw and wool blankets against the chill and leaking nappies. As she got ready for bed herself, Buttercup, her small farm dog, started to bark. She heard the pounding of hooves in her lane. She barred her door and peered out the shuttered window.

It was Palaver, the King's Man at Arms who brought her the quarterly pension.

"Ho, milady!" Palaver was gray-haired but hearty, a big man with a beard finely trimmed to show off his dimples. He was married to a much younger woman, the royal healer Fiona, a fiery little thing who had been her rock when she delivered Owen, squalling and healthy, in late winter. "Fiona sends her greeting. Is all well?"

"Hush, Buttercup. All's well." Her dog flopped down near the cradle and Morwenna opened the door to Palaver.

"Yes indeed, sir. We are fine here. Owen seems to grow overnight!"

"Excellent. I am here with a letter from the Queen." He handed her a scroll.

"From the Queen?" Morwenna stared at him in shock. She had never even spoken to her, though she had seen her riding through the shire, dressed in flowing foreign silks from her homeland of Padawar and surrounded by her Orc guardsmen. She always waved.

The letter was not done in a scribe's flowing hand, it looked like it had been written by Queen Tadame herself.

Dear Widow Morwenna of Bryce Longbowman, King's Guardsman,

I have a need of your services. Knowing how loyal your husband was to King Alerik, I hope my appeal will be met with your consent.

As you know, I brought from my homeland a company of Orcs to aid the King. They stood as loyal guards to me in these uncertain times.

Morwenna paused in her reading. Orcs? Why under the Blue Heaven would the Queen be writing to her, a widow with an infant, concerning Orcs?

My four loyal Orcs were poisoned five days ago, three are now dead. The remaining Orc, Sherrow, is an Orc by bite, not by birth. He is my cousin. Until his twelfth year, we were raised together in my father's palace. We were like brother and sister all our childhood. Since his change into an Orc he has always been my friend and protector.

This gave her pause. The Orcs were monsters, twice the size of an ordinary man, huge beasts of muscle with leather-like mottled olive, tan and gold splotched skin. Knife-sharp boar's teeth protruded from their jaws. She couldn't imagine one was once a human boy, or could be called friend.

I received a missive from a healer in my homeland. Sherrow can yet live! For this, he must consume mother's milk for a season, which will give his body enough sustenance to heal. Otherwise, he will die of starvation. Orcs are heavy eaters, as you can imagine. He can hold down nothing, not broth nor cow's and goat's milk. He is close to death as we speak, and there is not time to search for wet nurses. I asked Fiona, the healer, for suggestions of local women loyal to the King, who could possibly give milk to my dear cousin, and she mentioned you. You are healthy, with abundant milk, but more importantly, you are a woman of good understanding, not a silly, hysterical girl. And your husband was a Vallanhad Guard, loyal to King Alerik.

For this act of courage and kindness, you will be well rewarded with a lovely estate in the North, not far from your parent's home. You will have gold aplenty and the estate will bring you and your heirs a goodly income for generations to come.

Generations to come—Owen's future would be secure!

"Please send your reply back with Palaver. If you decide to care for my Orc he will be transported to your farm within the hour of receipt of your acceptance.

Sincerely,

Queen Tadame of Vallanhad

She looked up at the soldier. Palaver's eyes were kindly, crinkled at the corners, hallmarks of a life well-lived.

"Will Owen and I be safe?"

"Yes. He looks and fights like a monster, but thinks as a man. A good man."

She thought about that. "Can he understand me? And talk, with the tusks?"

"Sherrow had his tusks removed as a lad. He speaks our tongue well."

Her mind buzzed with thoughts.

"I will need more food and perhaps more rest to make large volumes of milk."

"That has already been determined. Fiona will accompany the carriage and will have food from the King's own pantry brought. There is also a page that can assist Sherrow with personal matters and bathing. You'll find Dudley to be a cheerful lad."

Morwenna wrote a reply on a small piece of parchment Palaver handed her.

An estate near my parent's home!

Palaver took to his steed and left a cloud of dust as the horse's hooves took her lane at a fast trot.

I hope I didn't make an awful mistake.

MORWENNA DOSED IN THE rocker by the fire when the party from the palace arrived much later that night. A common farm cart, driven by two plainly dressed men, no armaments visible, pulled into her yard. A boy about twelve sat in the rear of the cart, and the contents were covered by canvas as though to keep out the rain. Her stomach tightened. Was this going to bring danger to her and Owen? Someone had tried to kill this Orc. But who would know? Her nearest neighbors could not see her farmyard or lane due to a steep hillside and woods.

Palaver followed on horseback. "You are here alone, Mistress?"

"Yes sir, just me and my babe."

"The Orc is asleep. Fiona gave him a draught for the journey because the jarring on the road would be painful. His wounded stomach hurts."

She nodded. "I moved my table to make space for a pallet."

With that, the page, a boy plain of face, thick of build, and with a mass of curly blond hair, jumped out of the cart and began hauling wooden planks for a bed frame.

"This is Dudley, a page from the palace. He's a good lad."

The boy grinned, showing deep dimples, but continued unloading. Soon the three had a pallet crisscrossed with rope to hold a thick mattress, and then the Orc was carried into her cottage on a stretcher.

"The boy can help with your farm work. I must warn you he eats like a beast, but Fiona sent many goods. She will come here in the morning."

While they had been busy with the bed another cart pulled up, and the food items were brought in. Baskets of fruit, bags of oats and wheat flour, nuts, honey, hams, bacon and sausages were placed on her table and floor.

Morwenna was glad to learn Fiona would come by the next day. The sheer size of the sleeping Orc shocked her. His hands were the size of the hams now hanging from her rafter.

"Do not mention to your neighbors you are hosting the Orc. If he does well, we will transport you north to the estate in a fortnight. It is just a few miles from your parents' home. We are leaving a fast pony for the boy, in case you need help. And the lad is good with a crossbow."

Close to Mother and Father! She was fourteen days' journey from home now, and it was impossible to leave a small farm for that length of time. Her parents were also farmers, their inability to travel far was the same. Morwenna hadn't seen her mother since her marriage three years ago.

She had no time to dwell on that, though.

The Guardsman left.

"Come, Dudley. My cottage is so small I must have you sleep in the hayloft of the barn, but I think you will find it comfortable." Dudley grabbed a leather bag and his crossbow, which looked far too lethal for a young teen to manage. Morwenna carrying Owen and the oil lamp and took the boy to the barn. She showed him the hook for the lamp, and he clambered up to the hayloft. She was worried it would be too plain for the page, probably the son of a wealthy family being carefully trained in the palace. "I hope you are comfortable enough. There is quite a bit of hay, and those wool blankets are a tight weave so straw won't poke through."

"I will be fine, milady." He peered at her over the rail. "What is the mama cat's name?"

"That is Patches, she is friendly."

Dudley hopped down the ladder. "I will have company up there and I can make a comfortable bed on the straw. I will be very careful of the oil lamp and leave it on the hook. In fact, I doubt I will need it much. I have excellent night vision."

She grinned as the boy chattered on. His cheerful demeanor gave her ease and made her feel more comfortable about the Orc in her cottage.

Shortly after sunrise, as Morwenna cooked a large pot of porridge, four riders came up her lane. She recognized Fiona right away with her bright hair. Another woman accompanied her. She was dark-haired, dressed in leather leggings like a man. Morwenna had never met the Queen, but had heard of her exotic, tilted hazel eyes and thick dark hair. This must be Tadame.

Dudley made a sweeping bow, and she hurriedly made a deep curtsy.

"Your Majesty."

"Please call me Tadame. I thought it best to be here when Sherrow woke, since I am family."

"You are most welcome, Your Ma- Tadame."

They entered her small cottage, and she placed Owen on a blanket near the hearth with his collection of wooden toys. The other riders were guardsmen and remained in the yard.

"Your son is beautiful," Tadame said.

Morwenna felt her face heat. "Thank you. He is precious to me."

The Queen placed her hands on her flat belly. "I will have a child in the spring, Great Mother willing. They may be playmates at some time in the future."

Morwenna smiled but found it hard to see her child playing with a prince or princess someday. Fiona checked the Orc, who began to wake. His eyes, Morwenna was surprised to note, were the same hazel green as the Queen's, rimmed in dark lashes.

"Good morning, cousin. We have you safely hidden for now, and Goddess willing, will move you north out of harm's way in a few short days."

The Orc grimaced. "It was my job to protect you, Tad. Not be coddled like yon babe."

"You will one day be at full strength and protect me again. This is but for a season." She raised her eyebrows at him. "If it was a sword wound you would not fuss so much."

Sherrow scowled. "Honey bread pudding. I was laid low by a sweet."

Morwenna hid a smile. She did not expect an Orc to sound so much like a sulky child.

The Queen patted his shoulder. "A deadly disguise. You are staying with Morwenna. She is a young widow of one of the King's Guard, and has the babe who is not yet a year old. She has kindly agreed to share her baby's milk with you. How does your stomach feel this morning?"

"Still hurts. Out of breath." The words came out with an effort.

"This is our best plan to get you well."

The Orc nodded weakly and closed his eyes, but his lips curved into a smile. Morwenna noted that as a man he would have been handsome, with high cheekbones, a square jaw, finely carved full lips, and those eyes. What a pity he had been turned into a monster with mottled skin— though his face was mostly flesh-colored, with mottling along his temples. His arms, though. They looked like dragon skin.

The queen turned from the Orc's bed. "Dudley, show me the farm. It has been years since I was on a small steading."

"There are kittens in the loft."

"Perfect." The Queen and Dudley left the cottage.

"I thought it best to be here for the first drink of milk, to make sure it stays down. Though I have no other plan if it doesn't. But if you feel uncomfortable, I can leave," Fiona said.

"No, stay." Morwenna moved to the Orc's bed.

"Sherrow, meet Morwenna."

The Orc's eyes flicked over her for a moment, then closed again.

"I will endeavor not to frighten her."

"You take a short nap, Sherrow. I need to speak with Morwenna."

They sat at her table bench, Morwenna near the hearth. Fiona handed her a heavy silver mug.

"This mug is very old, and has been used in the King's nursery for centuries. It still has an enchantment on it. The milk will not spoil."

Morwenna swallowed hard as she took the small cup. A magical heirloom belonging to the King of Vallanhad— in her hand. They sat by her fire with her back turned to the Orc, and Morwenna filled the silver mug.

"I think he is asleep," Morwenna said a while later. They woke the Orc long enough for him to drink the warm milk. His eyes, such human eyes, had drifted shut after the few swallows.

"Yes, and he hasn't vomited. Tadame will be so relieved. Even a few sips of broth were returning right after he swallowed. This is excellent." Fiona went to the hearth and put Morwenna's kettle to boil in the coals. "You will need many fluids, and light labor. The boy Dudley will help. And if Sherrow gains strength we will head north very soon."

"We will? Are you coming, too?"

"Yes, Palaver and I and a handful of Guardsmen. We will leave before Midwinter."

She would see her parents at Midwinter!

"All this for the Queen's guard."

Fiona smiled. "Her cousin, actually. More like a brother, for they were raised together as children. She had a brother a little older than Sherrow, who disappeared mysteriously. It was a horrible tragedy. So she was devastated when Sherrow's father gave him to Orcs mercenaries to pay his debts just a year later, especially since the Orc bite causes a terrible fever that can kill. She did not learn until the following spring that he lived in the far north with an old Orc woman who took him from the Orc soldiers. Tadame asked the King for Sherrow as a guard as a gift on her wedding."

"So he lived with the Orcs until coming here with Tadame?"

Fiona pulled on her gray cloak, preparing to leave. "He was a castle guard a few short years before her marriage, and they spent time together quietly."

The Queen and Fiona left and the Orc slept. She helped the Orc drink two more cups of milk, while Dudley saw to her animals and cleaned the Orc while she took Owen out to play. That evening Morwenna fed Dudley ham and baked squash from her garden. "I hope you were comfortable in the loft. Make sure the doors are barred at night."

"I will. It was nice to be able to stretch out, and to not have to listen to other boys snoring all night."

She grinned at him. "Good. Come to the cottage as soon as you wake, and we'll have breakfast."

Morwenna put the bar across her door and sat by the fire to put more milk in the silver mug. The Orc was asleep. In the dim firelight, he looked entirely human, since the breadth of his shoulders was disguised by the down quilt covering him and the detail of his skin didn't show.

He had not thrown up. That was the best sign her milk would help him.

Chapter 2

SHERROW LOST COUNT of the days. He slept most of the time, waking for three feedings, which stayed down. A good sign he might live. During his waking times, Dudley cleaned him up like a giant baby but since he could not move his arms or legs more than a few feeble jerks, there was little he could do to change that embarrassing situation. He still needed help to sit up.

His thoughts often turned to his youth, the only other time he'd been incapacitated, after receiving the Orc bite. He couldn't recall how long he'd been bedridden then, but Perchka, who had stolen him away from the commander of the mercs he'd been sold to in repayment of his father's debt, had the ear of the King of Hobb. She adopted him as her son while he was still weak. It had all been less embarrassing with her because she was a powerful Erda, an Orc magic woman, and could do the bodily cleaning with magic. None of the changing and washing.

Dudley chatted about the farm work, the nanny goats and playing fetch with the small herd dog, Buttercup, while he cleaned Sherrow, seemingly unconcerned about the distasteful task. It did not lessen the boy's appetite, that was for certain. He ate like a teenage Orc, so much so Sherrow began to wonder if the boy didn't have Orc blood. Probably not, though, with those blond curls and fair skin. More likely some Lesser Giant blood there. The boy was only thirteen but stood two heads higher than Morwenna. The woman made simple meals of bacon or ham, eggs of different forms, cheese, and oatcakes with butter and jam, but she made a mountain of it, which the boy devoured.

"Who is your father, Dudley?" He asked one night, curious what noble family the boy came from.

"Duke of Amberwood. I'm the one and only heir. My Father is older and my mother died years ago, so Father and the King are happy to get me away from the palace and all the troubles."

"The Duke doesn't mind you doing farm work?"

The boy laughed. "Father is a bit unconventional. There are not many jobs on our estate I haven't helped with. Cleaning stables, laundry, baking, planting and haying. No linen mending. The ladies wouldn't let me help. But I have dyed wool. I've had weapon's training since I was little, so I'm ahead of the pages at the palace, plus I'm a lot larger. My father wants me well away from the palace since it is no longer safe."

SOMETIMES SHERROW WOULD hover between wake and sleep, the pain in his gut keeping him from drifting off. He would watch Morwenna through his eyelashes at those times, while she thought he slept. She was slim of build and moved gracefully through her small cottage, dark auburn braid swinging.

Her mouth fascinated him. Round, red like a cherry, an unusual shape that made him think of kissing. She had a mischievous smile for Dudley and her son, showing even white teeth, but she never smiled for Sherrow. He didn't expect her too, he was a monstrous Orc, after all. She looked at him with huge, light brown eyes, but she didn't seem afraid. Her child crawled to his bed and pulled himself to a stand, chuckling and crowing his triumph, and she didn't come running to rescue the babe. Instead, she praised the babe for his activity. He never heard her scold or screech. That was nice.

It was apparent mother's milk agreed with his ruined stomach, though he was still too weak to do more than gaze around the cottage. But before the milk he had been getting weaker, his breathing more shallow, heart skipping beats and making him light-headed, maybe on his way to death. Today he could draw in deep breaths, and though each breath still brought pain as his gut moved a little, it wasn't as sharp. His heart did a steady pound like it should, and he didn't feel odd beats or wake gasping for air.

He knew he was still near death because sometimes he caught a glimpse of Morwenna's firm breast when she fed the babe or squeezed milk into a mug for him. Her pink nipple didn't make him crazed with burning lust. When healthy, he was pretty much a raging fire of lust day after day, unsatisfied of course, except for rare encounters with camp followers desperate for coin. And Morwenna was lovely, with long shiny dark red hair, white skin with a few freckles over her nose, light brown eyes.

She was a womanly treasure, and not someone he would ever dare to court. No human woman would take him to wed now. And as comfortable as he was with Perchka's family, he could not imagine marrying an Orc wife. They married so young. What would he have to say to a fourteen-year-old Orc girl? The idea terrified him. Marriage was not for him.

THEY SOON ESTABLISHED a routine. Morwenna would feed the Orc early in the morning, and then Dudley came and helped bath him after he ate his own breakfast while the woman went out to work on the farm. Sherrow slept most of the time while Dudley and Morwenna did chores.

After several days Sherrow managed to sit up against the pillows with no help.

"Look at you sitting up! And you've been awake the whole time I've been here bathing you. You are getting better, milord!" The boy's sunny enthusiasm would have been annoying if it wasn't so genuine. That boy whistled and hummed all day long. Dudley the Cheery. Not a common trait among his fellow Orc Guards, though the hill folk he knew in his youth had been jolly.

The soldier Orcs had much joy knocked out of them at an early stage. If he was in charge of the army, things would be different. Why brutalize your own men?

He was stronger. Staying awake and sitting up, thinking about things, none of that had been possible even three days ago. "In the morn you will help me to the privy. I wish to cease this infantile treatment."

"Of course, milord!" The boy grinned at him and carried the bucket of slop water out to the garden. Sherrow slid flat with no help, though his arms felt heavy as he moved the pillows himself. He closed his eyes, knowing that rest would help him grow stronger. Deep inside a tiny flicker of what might be hope, glimmered. It seemed he would heal.

That evening Dudley went to bed early, a growth spurt no doubt fueled by the bushel of food he ate that day. Sherrow watched Morwenna bathe Owen in a large bowl. He grinned as the child grabbed her braid and dunked it in the water.

Watching her and her babe was pleasant. Peaceful. She bustled through the cottage and reminded him, oddly enough, of his Orc adopted mother, Perchka.

Well, they both had saved his life.

"You are regaining your strength," Morwenna surprised him by speaking to him as she dried the child off. "Until the past few nights, you were asleep by now."

"Yes. My plan is to start having Dudley drag me out to the privy. No more being a huge babe."

She actually grinned at that. The first time she ever smiled at him. His heart gave a tiny shudder.

"A worthy goal." She settled onto the small cot she slept on to nurse Owen. Since it was in a shallow closet he could not see much of her.

"You've been very ill before, I heard from Fiona. When you were bitten to be turned into an Orc."

"Yes. That was long ago, I was just turned twelve years. When Perchka came for me I had not had a drink of water in a day, I was too weak to ladle the water from a bucket. I had a high fever and none of the Orc soldiers would help me. They despised my father, you see."

He had a silver mug full of water right next to his bed, and was able to sip from it often. He often thought of that horrible day while he laid in bed.

"That is horrible."

"I was bitten in the southern borderlands of Hobb, not all that far from my father's estate in the Kingdom of Padawar. Perchka is an Erda, an Orc earth witch. Hobb is one of the Glister lands, like Vallanhad and Padawar. But Perchka is powerful. She had a vision of me, and came to save my life."

He yawned, the effort of speaking tired him. "It is a good story. I will tell you more on the morrow."

"Tell your story at dinner. I'm sure Dudley would enjoy it, also."

After supper the next day, Sherrow told his story. "The bite was on my neck, you can see the scar. It bled and I got a fever. The soldiers put me in a shed with a pile of straw, a blanket and a bucket of water with a ladle, to live or die. I was a human twelve-year-old, still a child, since I had not started my growth to manhood. Nothing like Dudley here, I was tall for my age but very thin. I weakened quickly. After a day I could no longer move enough to get a drink of water, or to relieve myself. I knew I was going to die. I woke to hear a woman's angry voice. 'I take the boy, you beasts with no honor', she screamed at the soldiers.

"I could see through gaps in the wall, a tall Orc woman in a cart pulled by four huge white narlhogs. She threw some sand or dust all around, then leaped out of the cart and rammed a tall wooden staff on the ground. The ground shook and a billowing cloud of glittery white filled the camp. Glister magic, like we have heard of from tales of old. I'd never seen it before since magic is gone from Padawar. When the cloud dissipated all the soldiers were unconscious on the ground. She grabbed a bag from her cart and came to me.

"'I am Perchka and I will take care of you', she told me. The first thing she did was give me water, from her own pouch, which was fresh and cool. Then she gave me potions in crystal vials, which took pain away, and bathed and changed me into clean clothes.

"'I live on a farm far to the north, and had a vision to rescue you and raise you as my son,' she said.

"I didn't understand anything about visions or magic, but I did not want to stay with those soldiers. I was so relieved. I told her I wanted to go with her, and that my name was Sherrow. She picked me up like a baby, placed me into a wooden cart full of straw and thick down quilts, and took me to her cottage in a valley surrounded by woods, many days journey from the soldier's camp."

"Did she kill all those soldiers with that magic?" Dudley asked.

"No, they went to sleep for a couple days, though. Long enough for us to get away and then go through a portal to her lands."

"Did you have to go back to them to be a soldier? They sound really mean."

"No. Perchka was a powerful Erda, a magic woman of the North. She knew the King. She arranged an education for me. Languages, economics, weapons training, history, geography, mathematics...The type of education I would have had as a noble youth back home."

"Those are things I have tutors for," Dudley said. "How come you don't have tusks?"

"Few Orcs in the north keep their tusks. Mostly the soldier clans who live in camps keep them. They make it hard to talk, to bargain in the market with visitors who are not Orc. So I had them pulled out after they came in."

"Perchka's cottage was not very unlike this one," he said. "The cottages in Hobb are round and built deep into the ground with steeply sloping roofs, so snow slides off. A fire always blazed and she cooked oatcakes with honey and fried fish or eggs and had a pungent hard cheese at every meal. She had a soothing ointment to put on my bite and herbs mixed in spirits to help me sleep.

"Eventually I healed and started growing into an Orc. Perchka just laughed and knitted clothes, simple wool leggings, tunics and capes, in browns and dull dark greens, unlike the rich jewel-toned velvets common for young boys back home. I enjoyed the freedom of movement of the Orc clothing while working the fields, hunting and fishing. Later I took weapons lessons from an Orc who had been a warrior long ago."

This woman Morwenna knitted with one stick while the babe played near the hearth. She loved her son and laughed and cooed at him. She was friendly with the boy Dudley, feeding him huge plates of food. Very much like Perchka, who had been kind to him.

"Your Orc village doesn't sound scary at all, Sherrow," Dudley said one night after a long discussion on hunting and fishing. "They are just like the villagers at home. But the Orc soldiers, they were terrifying."

"The Orc Guard live in camps from your age on. They are separated from regular people. The camps can brutal, depending on the commander."

"Did you have to go back to a camp?"

"No, I went straight from home to the King of Hobb's Personal Guard, and then to Tadame's guard duty back in Padawar. Then I followed her here. A diplomatic move."

THE NEXT DAY, MORWENNA, grinned as Dudley dragged the Orc out to her privy. Both were sweaty but there was an air of celebration when they returned. She made Dudley honey oatcakes with raisins.

Dudley had just devoured three bowls of porridge. He placed his bowl and spoon in her crockery washbasin and went to the Orc. Dudley helped the huge man up and bore half his weight out to the privy. Later they returned to the cottage and the Orc went immediately back to bed and fell into an exhausted sleep.

Morwenna gave Dudley an easy schedule of chores since it looked like hauling the Orc to the privy was exhausting work. Dudley headed out to the barn, and she spooned oatmeal gruel into her son, where it oozed out everywhere. Owen grinned, and she giggled, while Sherrow watched her move around the cottage with his unusual light eyes before asleep. Buttercup came into the house so Dudley must have the long-haired goats in the barn for their daily brushing. She kept the goats groomed as it made shearing and carding the wool so much easier.

Buttercup licked oatmeal from Owen's face to his giggling delight and then hopped up onto Sherrow's bed, for she adored him. Owen seemed to like him too, constantly crawling over to the bed to practice walking along it.

Fiona and Palaver came a few days later to check Sherrow's progress.

"He is walking to the privy twice a day," Dudley burst out with the pride of a doting parent.

"Then we will start him on bone broth and then calf's foot jelly. As soon as he can

hold down bone broth we will make plans to head north."

"What about my farm and all my animals? That is a long journey for goats in the fall."

"Dylan of Rogers died, leaving a widow with five children, three older boys and two small daughters. We thought to move them here."

"Oh. I remember Dylan and his family. I'm so sorry." Five children!

"I will send an envoy there tomorrow to get the caravan ready. Dylan's family can camp here for a bit before you leave so you can show them your routine. Luckily, the king has been persuaded to open the royal coffers to get Sherrow to safety," Palavar said. "There is livestock of all types on the north estate in the Borage Hills."

Fiona smiled. "The King loves Tadame so much. Her cousin means so much to her, he is willing to do whatever he can."

Chapter 3

FIONA BROUGHT BONE broth and calf's foot jelly in sealed pots. "Try this once a day, but only if it stays down. If you are in more pain or vomit after eating it, we'll wait another week."

Sherrow welcomed the broth and jelly, which he was able to tolerate, another sign he was getting better, even though he was still weak as a newborn kitten. He was determined to regain his strength.

One portion of his former vitality came roaring back soon after the increase in diet. *Just what is needed in this situation.*

It started one night when Owen woke. Morwenna changed him and stoked the fire, since the fall nights were getting cold. Sitting in front of the fire her hair gleamed burgundy in the firelight.

Owen popped off her nipple to whimper. Bare-chested, Morwenna murmured at her fussy child and ran a finger through Owen's mouth. Creamy rounded breasts, tinged with gold from the flames, dark nipples. Perfect roundness he longed to hold and kiss...

Sherrow froze on his bed. A molten river of desire rushed from somewhere deep within, making his formerly sleepy cock roar to life.

No. The last thing he needed to add to his current situation was lust for the sweet young mother who agreed to help him. He squeezed his eyes shut, but deep inside he knew it was no use. He was no sophisticated lover, flitting from woman to woman. He was an awkward soldier straddling two worlds, with only wealth to entice a wife. And he did not want a bought woman.

His future would be unrequited love for a lovely widow.

Goddess Above, he needed to get home to Hobb, to his castle, his people, his men at arms.

TADAME CAME FOR A BRIEF visit a few days before the caravan headed north, along with Palaver and Fiona.

"For the journey north I would like a small crossbow like Dudley has. I would like something I can use without tiring. All my weapons are for an Orc at full strength." Sherrow walked slowly through the farmyard with Tadame. The small journey left him shaky and exhausted, but he knew his strength would not return if he did nothing but rest.

"I can see that you get one. Not a bad idea, perhaps I will get one for myself. I was a good shot as a child," Tadame said.

"You were." Sadness seeped through him about Tadame. She loved her husband but could not really enjoy her life with him with his kingdom in turmoil.

"You should come with us, Tad. Surely Alarik wants you safe."

"He does, but my leaving Vallanhad right now would not secure a few of the border lords. Perhaps in the new year. Will you try to get back to Hobb?"

"Yes, I long for home." That was not all he longed for, but letting Tad know he had an interest in the widow would be actually painful.

"Your horses and weapons will be brought here in a few nights, so they can travel north with you."

They hugged goodbye. It could be a long time until they saw each other again. "Tell Alarik my castle and lands are safe for you and his heir. You should come as soon as you can."

"I will think about it. I hate to leave him, though."

"The time may come when he will be out on the battlefield. You can't go there. Come to Yllamar."

"I will, if it comes to that."

Sherrow sat outdoors on a bench for a long time after Tadame was no longer in sight.

Morwenna came out and put Owen on a small grassy spot under a tree.

"You will miss her."

"Yes. And I fear for her safety. I have tried to persuade her and Alarik to send her to Yllamar."

"What is that?"

"My estate in Hobb."

"You have an estate?"

Sherrow nodded. "I outlived my brother the heir, and my father, so I ended up with the lands in Padawar. I worked a deal, selling those lands back to the Crown since I did not want to live in Padawar. I petitioned the King of Hobb for lands. King Jonat of Hobb sold me Yllamar and also gave me the old northern riding. No one had been watching that border, so he was glad to have me."

"So you don't live in a cottage with a steeply sloping roof?"

"No. The castle is adequate. Perchka is my Regent while I am here."

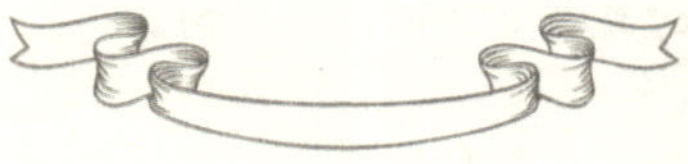

MORWENNA PACKED HER belongings in trunks and canvas bags. Most of the household items were staying in the cottage, her new home was fully furnished and the farm had out buildings and animals. She expected to feel sad to be leaving but instead she was excited. Back to the north, near her parents! Owen would grow up with grandparents, friends and relatives. Even while still a widow, she would not be all alone. She could not wait.

Sherrow was gaining some strength, though walking to the privy and a short stroll around the garden caused him to collapse in his bed for several hours. She hoped he would have a full recovery. He planned to go home, to Hobb, as soon as he could. She hoped he would winter with her, gaining strength, but she suspected he would leave before Midwinter. And he had an estate, with a castle, while she had been picturing him in a round cottage in the woods. It made sense though. Cousin to the Queen. Born into a noble house in Padawar. She would never have guessed that about an Orc.

She hoped he was well enough for this journey. A trip north, they could run into blizzards and frigid temperatures. Or days of rain that turned the roads to slop.

Morwenna forced herself to stop worrying. Plenty of travel happened before the dead of winter. Especially near Midwinter, when families traveled to relatives, and nobles went to their lands to see in a new year.

ONE NIGHT BEFORE THEY left they had a visitor.

"Father!" Dudley flew across the yard to a tall, sturdy man in fine clothes.

"I came to see you off, it will be summer or even later before I call you back home."

Dudley ushered his father into the cottage. "Father, this is Mistress Morwenna and Sherrow, an Orc Guard who is recovering from an injury."

The Duke of Amberwood gave a shallow bow to Sherrow, who nodded his head in acknowledgment. It was a bow meant for one of equal station.

"You are Margrave of the Northern March of Hobb," said the Duke.

"I am. Please sit down," Sherrow said Morwenna wondered if the man would sit on one of her humble wooden benches, but he did

"Then I greet you as an equal and request a boon," said the Duke.

"How may I be of service?"

"Dudley is my only son. My wife recently gave birth to twin daughters and as delightful as they are, they can't inherit should tragedy strike the House of Amberwood. I request that my son foster with you, at your castle in Hobb. This war...the noble houses are divided between King Alarik and his cousin the Duke of Redmond. It could go either way, and I fear it will be long and bloody. No environment for my only heir."

"I do intend to return to my lands of Yllamar and I would be honored to foster Dudley. I am quite fond of him."

"I am proud of my son. Though he does eat like a beast."

The Duke pulled a scroll from his cloak. "Mistress, I would like to have your name on here, also, as a witness of Dudley's guardianship papers. In these trying times I want to make sure my boy is staying with those I trust. I fear he and other children like him, the children of nobles who stand with Alarik, will be pawns in this war."

It was a sobering thought, children imprisoned or worse, to force concessions from the King. "I would be honored to help Dudley." Morwenna signed the document and also the copies she and Sherrow would keep.

The Duke tossed Dudley a leather pouch with the clink of metal. "Keep it hidden, and don't wear the Heir Apparent ring until you reach Hobb."

"Yes, Father."

"Now, come. Let me tell you of your twin sisters before I must leave." He wrapped an arm around his son. The two left the cottage.

Chapter 4

BUTTERCUP WOKE THEM by barking in the night they were to leave. The carts for the journey north pulled into the yard, quietly. Four guards on horseback helped them load their bags and crates, not that there was much since Morwenna's new estate would be fully furnished. Sherrow made sure his weapons were in the cart with the large bed he would rest on during the journey. It was a dark night, with just a sliver of moon, cold with a slight breeze. They all got settled into the carts and headed down the country lanes to the Great North Road. In an hour or so they joined the caravan.

"I am Baron Krutgar. I will be leading this caravan north. Are you settled? We will make a brief stop or two along the road but I plan to get to the Little Cut Road as soon as possible. We will camp there, rest up and then press north." The Baron was a tall, thin man, finely dressed, with a pointed beard.

Sherrow was not familiar with the Little Cut Road. He traveled to Hobb on the Great Road East and hadn't traveled north in Vallanhad.

"Dudley," he barked. "You travel with Morwenna. And keep a knife and your small crossbow near."

"Yes, sir."

"You, driver. We will follow directly behind the lady's cart, do you understand?"

"Yes, sir." The old man smelled of strong drink, but that was true of most old soldiers, with a lifetime of injuries causing pain.

"Watch for any soldiers that come to bother Morwenna. Whistle for me if you suspect trouble," Sherrow told Dudley.

Dudley had a piercing whistle.

"Oh. All right." Dudley frowned a moment. "What do you plan to do to them?"

Sherrow shrugged. "I'm pretty confident I can make any one of them eat rocks before my strength gives out."

Dudley grinned. "I'll help. But I think this lot is all right. Mostly old guys, looks to me."

The weather was cold and crisp, with no rain. Morwenna was glad to see the sky was clear. Traveling with a baby, sleeping nights in a cart, she was hoping for good weather all the way home. Fiona had assured her the down quilts and furs would keep them warm, but she was still concerned. She had Owen all bundled up, with a fur-lined leather cap covering his ears.

Morwenna, Owen and her dog were given one cart with a canvas top, driven by an elderly soldier. The trail master, Baron Krutgar, pushed hard to get in as many miles as possible in good weather. Morwenna decided they were taking the less popular road for safety purposes. The Orc assassin had not been found.

Well into the afternoon before they came a narrow road forking off to the west. Here they stopped for a meal. Morwenna joined Sherrow and Dudley in Sherrow's cart

"Where is the healer and her husband?" Sherrow asked Dudley who served him a cup of milk, still warm, and a pot of calf's foot jelly. "We have not yet seen them."

"I'll walk through the camp and look for them."

Dudley came back in a short while.

"They aren't in the camp. I didn't see a single King's Guardsman that I know, and I am pretty familiar with them since I lived at the

Palace. I had weapons training with them." His face was serious, an expression not often seen on his young face. "I think Morwenna is the only woman in the whole caravan."

Sherrow was furious. "I think the caravan was hijacked. There should be Guards we know, and Palaver should be here. Dudley, you will stay with Morwenna all day and if the others try to order you around, ignore them. And carry a knife at all times, both of you. A change of plans with an assassin on the loose calls for extra caution."

She caught his eyes, and he nodded at her. "I have my weapon's chest here. Are all your weapons in the cart or packed with the household goods, Dudley?"

"My longbow and arrows are packed."

"Get them in the cart when we camp for the night." He opened his chest and handed Morwenna a dagger. "This is elf made. It rarely misses."

"Wear your small crossbow at all times." Dudley strapped on his crossbow.

"Driver." Sherrow spoke sharply and the old man turned to him with wide eyes. "Go get Baron Krutgar."

Baron Krutgar arrived as they were getting ready to move out. "What is going on? We are ready to move."

"Where is the healer and her husband?"

"Well, there was a change of plans. My company was ready to head north since this band of soldiers have orders to the north border station. Since we are trying to stay ahead of the weather, you were sent north with us. The healer could not make it. Perhaps she will follow you north. Now, get situated, we will be moving in a few minutes."

"Why do they need soldiers at the north border? Those mountains border Giant lands, but they are nearly impenetrable. There is no pass." Morwenna said after he left.

"I have never heard of this Baron. Palaver should have been the ranking leader of the caravan. Something is not right. We have our weapons, that is good. Morwenna, I think you and Owen need to sleep in this cart with me. I know it will be crowded, but safety has to be our priority. We will have Dudley and the dog in the other cart, parked right next to us." Sherrow frowned. "You, ah, don't need to worry about my behavior. I am a gentleman. Plus I will be keeping watch."

Morwenna shifted sleepy Owen on her lap, disquiet tightening her stomach. *Not safe.* "The whole point of going north was to get you to a safer place. Can we turn back?"

Sherrow looked her in the eye before dropping his gaze. "No. If there are enemies in this group we would be even more vulnerable, and I do not have my strength back for a fight. And where would we go?"

That night as Morwenna prepared to sleep, planning to slip over to Sherrow's cart after the drivers left for their tents, she heard the stamp of horses hooves. It was a soldier, a major she thought.

"I am Major Winfield. Baron Krutgar sent me by to show the page his quarters."

Maybe they are after Amberwood's heir!

"Dudley will stay here with me."

"That is not seemly, mistress. He will have to bed down with the other soldiers."

"Don't tell me what is seemly! He is with me to help care for the Orc. He might be needed in the night. The boy will remain here."

The man leaned close. "Look, these are orders from the Baron. He is in charge of this caravan."

"I have papers. The page is not in service to the King. His father has an agreement with the Orc."

"With the Orc! Nonsense!"

"Go get your Baron." Sherrow spoke from the cart nearby.

"Sherrow has extensive lands in Hobb. My father wants him to foster me." Dudley's usually cheerful demeanor was replaced by an angry look.

"I'll go get the Baron."

"You do that," Morwenna retorted.

Baron Krutgar soon arrived on horseback, looking disgruntled.

"I have guardianship papers for the boy." Sherrow handed the parchment to the Baron, who read them with the help of an oil lamp held by the Major.

"I see." The Baron rolled the parchment up and handed it back to Sherrow. "The boy stays with the Orc. The papers were signed by his father, the Duke of Amberwood."

"You are Amberwood's heir." The Major looked a little ill.

"I am. And my father wants me to foster with Sherrow." Dudley raised his nose in a snooty manner, all high-born offense.

"Now, can we all get back to our rest?" The Baron turned and rode away, the Major following.

"That is settled." Dudley moved Morwenna's bedding to Sherrow's cart.

"This is going to be very crowded," she said as she entered his cart. He was huge and already took up most of the space.

"I plan to take a half-night watch, then Dudley will be on watch. We will both need some sleep time during the day. So I will be sitting here to keep watch, not on the bed with you." Sherrow had a flap cut in the canvas to watch the road behind them.

"All right."

"I doubt any of the soldiers will know you are sleeping in here, since we are parked away from the tents."

"Yes. Well, it also solves one of my worries. I was afraid I would not be able to keep Owen warm, but with two adults we should be warm enough."

"I can keep a small oil lamp lit, while I am awake. Under the canvas it will warm the air."

She settled on her down mattress and pulled a down quilt and bearskin over her and Owen, who was sound asleep. It did not feel as intimate as she had imagined, since Sherrow was sitting, leaning against the side of the cart and peering through a hole he'd made in the canvas.

"I wonder about the estate. I know some farm workers headed there with goods and stock animals when you were first brought to the cottage. But Fiona and Palavar were to stay with me until spring."

"We will assess the situation when we arrive. If I can get to Hobb I can send workers and guards to you. Or you could stay with your parents until the situation is stable."

"Traveling to Hobb is a long journey, and in the winter!"

Sherrow gave an amused snort, "Perchka gave me a most valuable gift. Magic remains alive in Hobb, unlike in Vallanhad. We have a type of portal magic. Mother learned it in a journey to the East in her youth. My journey to Hobb will only be a day or so."

Morwenna thought about that for a while. "Vallanhad lost its magic before I was born. I wonder why?"

"I do not know. My original homeland, Padawar, still has a little magic, but it is rare and weak. Hobb has magic, the Giant lands do, too. Our neighbors to the west, the north land of Frost does, but the lands across the sea from them, your neighbors to the west, are like Padawar, with some magic, but it is rare. The lands to the Far East, Emrysdell and Hoightlund have magic."

"It is odd to think that if I lived in my great-grandmother's day, I could have worked magic. My grandmother would tell me stories of her mother and grandmother doing Glister magic when I was little."

"The old women say that someone, or a group of mages, worked arcane magic which has stopped the Glister magic. But Perchka says that is only speculation, no one has proof something like that happened."

"If they could find the reason they could bring it back?" To be able to use Glister magic was a dream she'd had since childhood.

"In Hobb we have seen immigrants regain their magic, though they are untaught. My mother wishes to start a school, to find and save the old magic knowledge." Sherrow paused. "I have been away from my lands for too long. My mother stands as regent, but while overseeing my responsibilities she cannot move forward with her school."

"How long have you been here?"

"Nine months. I hate to leave Tadame. But I think the king will send her to my castle in Hobb, to keep her and the heir safe."

"What is your castle like?"

"It overlooks a lake. It is very large, with thick walls, and one wall is built into the mountain. There are miles of caves."

She snuggled Owen close. It had never occurred to her that Orcs had castles, and magic. Or even schools. Hobb neighbored her country, and yet she knew so little about the land.

"Owen went to sleep easily."

Morwenna laughed. "I thought traveling might be difficult with an active baby, but Owen has discovered he can throw things out of the cart. Dudley got him a basket of twigs, and he spent the afternoon throwing them out the cart. Dudley promised to fill the basket with more sticks for tomorrow."

By the dim light of the oil lamp, Sherrow found himself watching the woman sleep rather than watching the camp. Her hair was caught in a loose braid and strands fell around her face. In the firelight her skin looked impossibly smooth and soft. He wanted to touch her. He'd touched her hands before, accepting a mug or handing Owen to her. He'd never touched her hair, or the silken skin of her throat, and he longed to.

It was a good thing he wasn't stretched out just inches from her. He wasn't sure he could refrain from stroking her hair or face.

A WEEK PASSED WITH no threats. Sherrow urged them to remain vigilant, because they still couldn't trust the caravan. At night, he took watch, though it had stayed quiet.

He turned his face back to the slit and watched the caravan for movement every night. They were camped in a wooded area tonight, more cover for hiding.

He had a secret, though Dudley was in on it. He'd been eating bread and cheese once a day, and could keep it down. There was pain, but even with that, he felt strength returning with the heavier food. That was a secret he wished to keep. He wanted the soldiers in the camp to think three pulls on his longbow wore him out. He made a point of leaning against a tree and then walking slowly to his cart for a nap. Let them think he could barely move.

Tomorrow he would double his food intake.

THIS JOURNEY WAS TO be two weeks long, longer if they ran into bad weather and had to camp for a few days along the road. Morwenna hoped that wouldn't happen and that the fine weather would hold, but they were only five weeks from midwinter. She did not want to be out on the road with an infant and a sick Orc in a snowstorm. How she hoped they would be safe in her new home, with her mother and father joining them, before the north winds turned icy.

Much of the scenery on their journey was beautiful, and she had few responsibilities other than caring for her son and feeding the Orc. Mornings were cold and the ground was white with frost. There had been a few drifting snowflakes, but nothing like the thick snowfalls of her childhood. Maybe they would be all right. Sherrow seemed to be gaining strength on her milk in a cup, and eating the fine ground oat gruel she fed to Owen once a day. Dudley told her it gave him an awful stomach ache, but he insisted.

When they stopped for the midday meal Sherrow worked with Dudley to shoot his bows, and several of the soldiers in the company joined them. She noticed Sherrow was rarely beaten in the shooting matches, and Dudley improved quickly.

Owen adored the Orc, hollering for 'Airwo' whenever he saw Sherrow. Sherrow gave the babe piggyback rides, carefully holding his short legs so Owen wouldn't flop backward.

Sherrow no longer looked like a monster to her. His face was human and expressive. His eyes would light up when he saw her and when he smiled his teeth gleamed white and strong. He was larger than all the other men, with broad shoulders and slim hips and much of his skin was that rough texture and color, like snakeskin. Owen liked to rub his hands over Sherrow's arms. She thought it might make Sherrow self-conscious but he had laughed at the little boy. "Tough like dragon skin, rahrrr," he joked with Owen. Then he would fly Owen through the air in his large hands which made Owen squeal and laugh.

SHERROW WAS FEELING better. His food plan was working. He wasn't at full strength, but he was getting stronger every day. He thought he could probably do the journey on horseback, but the enforced rest of riding in a cart was probably good for him. He spent part of the time lifting and lowering his broadsword, hidden under the canvas roof, to strengthen his arms. His stomach still hurt at times, but he was able to keep the food down, and he could walk a small distance as they headed north. He also spent less time napping and generally sat up in the cart and watched the road.

Normally he watched the trail ahead of the caravan, with sweeps through the caravan to see what the men were up to. One morning they had passed a lovely small lake, so he turned around in the cart to watch it through the wide open flap as they moved away from it. Back in the distance, he saw the glint of metal in sunlight. He refocused his eyesight to see long distances. As an Orc he could use far-sighted vision when he wished. This was an ability that the Orc guards had kept to themselves because it was good to be underestimated.

He watched for an hour as they were traveling through heavy woods. He occasionally caught a glimpse of metal, but that was all.

Perhaps it was the King's Guard and the Healer who had not shown up for the journey as planned.

They halted for lunch, he ate gruel and a cup of warm mother's milk. Dudley placed a large bread roll with cheese and bacon under his blankets, to eat while he 'slept.' When they rolled again, there was a turn in the trail and there before him, perhaps a day's travel away, was a steep-walled canyon.

Just the place for an ambush.

Sherrow folded up the blankets and made a pile with his pillows, so he could slump on them, appearing to others to be resting, but actually he could see over the wall of his cart, toward the back of the company. The now steep path had a break in the thick woods with a clear view to the south. He focused his eyes for distance.

A company of twenty armed men, traveling light with no carts, kept pace with the caravan. He suspected they received food from the cook wagon, since he saw no carts with provisions. Which meant Baron Krutgar and the soldiers were aware of the followers. They were about two miles behind them, hidden from anyone without a spyglass or Orc eyes.

Soldiers behind them, a narrow canyon, soldiers all around, no King's Guard...

"Dudley, I need to talk to you and Morwenna, now!"

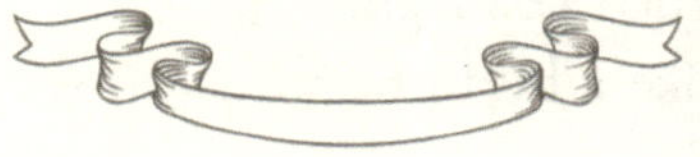

DUDLEY CAME BOUNDING up to her cart, out of breath. "Milady, Sherrow needs to speak to you, right now. He wants both of us."

A chill ran through her. Was he ill? He had been eating oat gruel three times a day, and she thought he was getting better, because he often sat up in his cart and watched the scenery, and was far more active than he had been at first. Heart pounding, she handed Owen to Dudley and climbed out of the cart. She was no healer, she only knew Sherrow was recovering from a deadly poison, what if she couldn't help him? She shivered as a chill of fear ran down her spine.

Sherrow was sitting up and looking healthy. His odd skin no longer had a gray cast. Most of it was a warm flesh tone, though along his temples and the sides of his throat the flesh was olive and tan patches, and a thick rougher texture. His arms were also textured, and she had heard him tell Dudley his Orc skin was harder to pierce with an arrow or blade.

"You wanted to see us?"

"Yes, join me in the cart."

"Driver, why don't you take this coin and see if the cook won't draw you an extra pint."

The old man caught the tossed coin deftly and hurried off with a grin.

Dudley resumed his seat up front and got the cart rolling. Owen giggled as Buttercup licked his face

"There is a little-known fact about Orcs I wish to explain to you." Sherrow paused while they both frowned at him. "Look at my eyes." They did so and he changed to distance vision. His pupils changed to slits and his eyes turned a dark gray.

"Hunt sight. Like a bird of prey. I can see long distances that humans cannot see."

"What do you see?" Morwenna had a bad feeling, built on her unease about the missing guardsman and healer; she reached for her baby.

"We are coming to a narrow canyon, a place for easy ambush." He frowned at her. "Is this the road you have taken in the past to your home?"

"No, I've always traveled on the Great North Road and then taken the Blue River Road which goes near my home, which goes west of the North Road."

Sherrow nodded. "A company of twenty armed men is following us, at a distance humans cannot see. We will reach a narrow canyon tomorrow."

"We are surrounded by traitors?" Morwenna looked straight into the Orc's eyes.

"I believe so. I think we should leave this caravan tonight. We'll have to go overland. I think we are ...expendable, and the estate up north will make a good stronghold for the rebels. Plus, they will have the Duke of Amberwood's heir as hostage."

Morwenna took a deep breath. "I see."

"Dudley, I need you to get provisions for us, some of those dried meat and berry biscuits, water bags, packed into saddlebags. We will need to leave tonight, before we get to that canyon. We can't take a cart. My horse and my pack horse are with the stock."

"My gelding is with the stock animals also." Dudley said.

"So we need our horses and gear. Morwenna can ride my pack horse, he is sturdy and reliable. You get the provisions together, Dudley. Morwenna pack for you and the babe. I can rig the bearskin as a holder for the baby while you ride."

"Where will we go?" Morwenna asked.

"Luck was with us, for a change. We will head southeast, overland through the foothills. We are near the eastern border of Hobb, we can be there in a day. We will go there and regroup."

Chapter 5

DUDLEY SPENT THE AFTERNOON slipping about the camp liberating supplies and saddle bags. Dudley brought the driver another pint of ale, so the old man was half asleep as they followed the road. Morwenna packed her belongings into the saddle bags, and they joined together quietly after the evening meal, both their carts closed up so others couldn't see inside. Sherrow looked at Morwenna. She wore a warm woolen gown and a farm wife's footwear, leather clogs with wood soles, not meant for the trail.

"Dudley can you find her some boots? And woolen trousers. The gowns won't work well since we'll be traveling through thick woods. Yours won't fit her, though. What about that skinny page?"

"Ainsley? His boots should about fit. Plus, he'll be at the campfire sneaking ale."

"Go get them."

Dudley took off.

Sherrow turned to Morwenna. "Do you have your slingshot and stones?"

She nodded. She had used it back on the farm to keep the weasels away from her chickens.

"Keep it handy. We don't know what we might encounter on the road."

He handed her the heavy, bearskin rug. "This will come in handy if it snows. It will keep you and Owen dry." He had fashioned it into a carrier she would wear around her neck and waist, Owen safely tucked to her front.

Dudley returned in a short while, with clothing and a pair boots for Morwenna. "These are his dress boots."

Morwenna quickly pulled on the man's shirt and leather tunic, with two pairs of woolen pants for warmth under her skirt. She adjusted Owen in the leather pouch and threw her heavy woolen cloak and hood on top.

"Quiet now. Is Owen asleep still?"

"Yes." They quietly made their way along the wooded edge of the camp to where Sherrow had the horses hidden. Buttercup was lifted into a basket tied to the back of Dudley's saddle since Morwenna refused to leave the dog alone with the caravan.

She was scared but felt safer with Sherrow and Dudley than with the Baron or his men.

Sherrow and Dudley placed leather boots on the horses to muffle their hooves. "We will not be able to move swiftly at first, the horses have less purchase on the rocky ground. I'll lead. Dudley, bring up the rear and have your crossbow at the ready," Sherrow whispered.

They made way through the scrubby woods alongside the path. Morwenna was tense, expecting to hear from someone at the camp, but though she could hear voices from the campfire, no one noticed their leaving. Owen was sound asleep in the sling she wore, covered up from the cold night air.

Sherrow slowed to a stop and they joined him. "The followers are not far from here, but I want us to cross the road to that wooded hill, so we don't pass any closer to them."

They did, walking their horses up the hill and eventually down the other side. Sherrow and Dudley removed the leather boots from the horses. After that Sherrow had them press faster through the dark woods.

They traveled until dawn, pushing as hard as they could with only a few breaks. The sky began to lighten. Morwenna kept drowsing, then jerking awake. Owen woke once in the night, and she had to stop to change him, and then nursed him back to sleep.

They stopped for a few minutes at dawn to rest the horses. Dudley handed her a mug full of small cubes of soft cheese and oatcakes which she shared with Owen after they mounted again, while she followed Sherrow through thick, dark woods.

Late in the morning Sherrow stopped and got off his horse. "I'll be right back." He slipped into the trees and Morwenna soon lost sight of him.

He returned a short time later. "We're being pursued, they are not far behind us."

Sherrow's quiet voice sent terror racing through her.

"Dudley, see that hill with the rock outcrop? Ride there as fast as you can and set up with your longbow. It will soon be dawn, you will have the best view."

"Yes, sir."

"Morwenna, you follow Dudley but stay on the downslope of that hill, out of the line of arrows. Dudley, watch for the glint of metal and target them. Do your best to hit them, and make sure you have cover. I will join you as soon as possible."

Dudley took off, and Morwenna turned to follow, holding Owen tight with one arm.

"Milady," Sherrow said. "You need to go, now. I'm sorry to bring you this trouble. I had hoped to keep you safe."

She pulled her horse close to him. "I am worried about you fighting those men."

"I will be fine, Morwenna. I am stronger than you know. And I am so sorry."

"Shh." She placed a finger over his lips. "None of this is your fault. You have tried so hard to keep us safe." She leaned down and brushed her lips against his.

Sherrow was stunned. Frozen in place. She kissed him. Him! Without thought, he pulled her closer, kissing her back. His kiss wasn't a sweet brush of lips, though, but a hard, wild kiss of desire. Heat burned through him and all he could think of was her soft warm lips, her small tongue meeting his, her scent...

"Sherrow, we must go." Morwenna pulled back and Owen kicked at him, wiggling in his pouch.

"Yes. I'm sorry."

She smacked his shoulder. "I'm not." She grinned, and he found himself joining her in a shared smile.

"Here." He pulled the leather pouch of ward stones from his belt.

"Take these. If the ambush should succeed and I do not come up the ridge to you by full sunrise, take Dudley and flee southeast. Even if they win this skirmish I am sure I will slow them down. In half a day you will be in the land of Hobb. Any Orc along the way, or cottage or farm, show them these ward stones. They can fetch my mother. My adopted mother, Perchka will take care of you all."

"You are going to try to fight them all?"

"Dudley has his longbow." He pulled out his sword, which was almost as long as she was tall. She'd seen him use it many times, parrying gently with Dudley. But now the blade wasn't gleaming Orc silver, but a dark, dull gray with splotches of brown. She stared at it and then looked at Sherrow.

"Orc stealth steel. Dudley knows about it. Any steel catching light will belong to them. He can estimate where the soldier is. And my skin and clothing repel arrows."

He lifted a hand to her face and traced her upper lip. The gentle touched sent a rush of heat through her.

An overwhelming desire to kiss him again, to show him he was worthy, filled her. She gripped his face between her hands and pressed a deep, warm kiss on his lips while he held still as stone before gathering her into his arms for a moment.

They broke apart. "You are a good man, Sherrow."

"Take care, Morwenna." He turned his steed and moved away from her.

She shifted Owen around; he was awake and starting to fuss, until he could find her full breast, and headed the horse toward the hill. Once there she tied her horse next to Dudley's, grabbed her leather satchel and struggle uphill to the boy.

"See anything yet?" She spoke softly.

"Not yet."

Morwenna pressed trail cakes into his hand and then got Owen changed. She fed him a few bites of a soft cheese and shared a pouch of water with Dudley.

"There," he breathed.

She handed Owen his horse with the rope mane and tail and peered over the large rock Dudley had set up behind. She saw movement down below in the woods.

Dudley sent an arrow twanging through the cold morning air. *Don't let it hit Sherrow.* She wasn't a believer in the gods, but it couldn't hurt, right?

Owen was making plenty of noise, talking to Buttercup and his toy horse. She hoped his babbling wouldn't carry down to the armed men. There was no point in shushing him, Owen didn't understand being quiet yet.

Dudley shot another arrow, and then a barrage of them, so fast she couldn't even count. Sherrow had worked with him on speed. She peered over the rock but saw nothing. A zing of an arrow passed right by her, and she yanked Dudley down, throwing herself over her son. The arrow continued past them into the woods.

"Someone knows we are here."

Dudley nodded, his freckles showing stark against his fair skin. "Is it time to go? Maybe we should head out."

She looked at the overcast sky. "Maybe. It is hard to tell how much time has passed."

"There are lots of swords in one area. Let me shoot a bit longer. It will help Sherrow out."

"All right. I will watch the hill."

"We're going to ride on the horsie again," she told her son. She crouched down and rushed back to the horses, who were lower on the hillside so out of line with the arrows. She untied her horse and got them situated. Owen pulled his toy up and showed it to her. She tied it with twine from her bag to the pouch, so she didn't have to keep retrieving it from the ground. "Smart boy."

Buttercup was nearby, she would alert them to any soldier coming. Morwenna readied her slingshot with a stone.

Buttercup leaped up barking and charged down the hill. Morwenna rushed after the dog in time to see a soldier swipe at the small dog with his sword. Buttercup dashed away just in time.

Not my dog, you ass. She whipped her sling and let loose. They were only thirty feet apart. She could hit much smaller targets at a longer distance. The stone hit him on the nose with a satisfying crunch. He dropped, blood flowing from his broken nose. She followed with a second stone to the head, hoping it would knock him out. It did.

"Dudley come on!"

He scrambled down the hill to the horses and mounted. "I hate leaving him."

Dudley nodded. "But I think he is stronger than anyone knows. He has been pretending to be weak. He thought all along something was wrong. There were no more sword flashes."

"I thought he might be pretending a little, after Fiona and Palaver failed to join us." Hearing Sherrow might be stronger than he looked was reassuring.

They traveled through the forest over two hills, stopping at a small creek to water the horses and get Buttercup into of her carrier behind Dudley's saddle after a drink. They pressed on to the southeast.

Where is Sherrow? There was no sound of battle or of horses in pursuit.

The morning had started with clouds to the west, they thickened, becoming heavy snow clouds and obscured the sun, so she couldn't tell how close they were to midday. Fluffy flakes drifted down, melting as soon as they touched the ground. Owen was content to slobber on a baby oatcake. The heavy bearskin cloak and his woolen layers kept him warm enough as long as she kept him changed and dry.

Hopefully, they could stay the night at a farm.

And Sherrow would find them.

Buttercup started barking. Dudley leaped off his horse and let the dog down. She tore off up the hill they had just traveled over.

"Get into the trees," Dudley said and Morwenna urged her horse into a thick stand. Dudley grabbed his short crossbow.

"It is I, Sherrow," a voice rang down to Morwenna and Dudley. "Don't shoot."

"Sherrow!" Dudley lowered his weapon and ran up the hill.

Sherrow had a bloody cut on his chin and a rag wrapped around his left forearm, but otherwise looked unharmed. Morwenna rushed to his side, only Owen in his sling preventing her from throwing her arms about him. Sherrow grabbed her tight with one arm, Dudley with the other.

"You are injured?" She asked.

"Just a cut."

"What about those men who attacked us?" Dudley asked.

"Those that live are tied to their horses. I will bring them. Dudley, your shooting was most successful. Many of the men sport arrow wounds. It made it easier to take them down."

Sherrow moved down the hill, holding his horse's reins. A trail of horses tied behind followed him. The soldiers were tied hanging head down on their horses. A few stirred, some had bloody wounds.

"Stay away from them. I will have them trail behind us several feet so there is no chance for trouble. Though I doubt they can get loose. Dudley, if you would pull up the rear. If any stir, let me know and I will knock them out."

Morwenna and Owen got back on her horse, and Dudley buckled the tired dog into her basket.

They traveled a few more miles, Dudley and Sherrow speaking of their actions in the battle. Owen napped for a bit and Morwenna nearly dozed in the saddle, so relieved. She was with mesmerized by the fat snowflakes, exhausted from the long night and the battle.

Sherrow came to her and they halted. "My ward stones?" She pulled them out of the bag on her belt.

"Are you all right, Sherrow? Do you need to eat?"

"I am eating some of Owen's baby biscuits." He handed one to Owen. "Share with me, Owen."

Owen gave him a slobbery grin and took the biscuit.

Sherrow drew a finger down her cheek. "I think the milk days are over. I will eat the bread and cheese Dudley has packed."

"But won't it hurt your stomach?"

"I have been eating bread and cheese for days. There is still discomfort, but I am getting better." Sherrow grinned.

He ate while walking around. "We are in Hobb. I am bonded to this land and already feel stronger. My ward stones?"

Morwenna handed him the pouch and he took the ward stones out of the bag. He whispered an incantation over them, and then he tossed them. They landed in a perfect circle and began to glow.

"You will follow me into the circle. It will take us to my estate, Yllamar, in the north. Bundle up, it will likely be full winter there."

He turned to the men tied to their horses. "Ho, traitors. We will be in my lands in minutes. Don't worry, your horses will soon reside in a warm stable, and you'll have a residence in my dungeon."

Sherrow mounted his horse and led them into the circle of stones.

Chapter 6

WHEN THEY ENTERED THE circle, Sherrow got off his horse and arranged the circle to a larger size to hold the prisoners. After making sure all were in the circle, he bent down and touched a glowing stone. "Home."

The surrounding air swirled but there was no pressure. It thickened into a white mist, with the glittering lights of Glister. Morwenna clutched Owen tight. Magic! Something she had never expected to see.

It tingled as it touched her skin. Owen giggled and tried to grab handfuls of the sparks. Buttercup ran around the horses, tail wagging. The horses didn't seem upset. The mist disappeared, and they were overlooking a snow covered valley with gentle snow drifting down. High, rocky hills surrounded the valley.

"Turn around."

Morwenna turned her horse. A castle rose on a rocky outcrop on a lone mountain, so high she had to tip her head back to see the top of the spires. Beyond it was another valley with an ice covered lake.

"Welcome to Yllamar, my castle. Let us get inside."

He took his Orc sword and stabbed it into the ground. Far away at the castle she saw the drawbridge come down. And it kept coming, rolling down the rough dirt trail to Sherrow, who had moved to the front of the group. From the castle a band of Orc soldiers thundered toward them. Soon they were met with shouts and laughter.

Instead of a long steep journey to the castle, the path somehow leveled, and they quickly approached the castle. Magic of some sort,

Morwenna thought. She allowed Sherrow to lead her horse through a gate to a wide courtyard bustling with activity. Sherrow was immediately thronged by a crowd of Orcs, humans, and some others she did not recognize, that were not Orc or human. Dwarves, perhaps. Some had rabbit ears.

"My people, there will be a feast tomorrow tonight, bring your families. But for now I need to get my party settled. Captain, with me. Have your men put the prisoners in the fourth dungeon and stable the horses with care," Sherrow ordered.

They were escorted into the castle, through an enormous Great Hall and up a flight of stairs to a small dining area. Soon they were seated at a long table. Hot mulled cider was placed before them by a young Orc woman who directed Morwenna to the personal room. Morwenna found her way to a room with toilet facilities and warm water in a basin. She got herself and Owen cleaned up a bit, braiding her hair and washing both their faces. Back in the dining room plates of roasted meat, cheese and bread had been served, along with fruit tarts, red wine and ale. She fed herself and Owen while Sherrow left them to talk to his Captain of the Guard.

An elderly Orc women came into the hall. She wore plain clothing and carried a thick staff. Sherrow greeted her with an embrace and Morwenna knew that must be Perchka. Sherrow brought her to the table.

"Mother, this is Morwenna, who kindly nursed me while I was ill, her son Owen, and Dudley, who is now a page here at Yllamar," Sherrow said. "I have a bit more business with my Captain but will join you soon."

Sherrow and the Captain left the table and stood in the doorway of the room. Perchka joined Morwenna at the table and poured a stein of ale.

"How do you do, Madame?" Morwenna asked. She smiled at the woman but couldn't keep from watching Sherrow. Surely he was exhausted.

"I have had few days as good as this one." She followed Morwenna's gaze to Sherrow. "But I suspect we will need to make Sherrow rest. He is not quite recovered, is he?"

"I am sure he is exhausted. We rode through the night, then he battled a group of soldiers."

Sherrow and the Captain left. Morwenna ate and drank the strong ale.

Perchka grinned. "Well, the soldiers are in the dungeons now. Are you finished eating? Come with me. You too, boy with golden curls." They followed her up the stairs to a gallery.

"Here we are." Perchka opened the door to a sitting room of great wealth, with windows of glass panes and cut crystal arranged in a pattern, letting in light. "The Lady's Suite. You will find a bath and bed in the adjoining rooms. I will have a cradle sent up and a maid will come to attend you and the babe. Rest. You will be called for the supper."

"Yes, Madame."

"And you, my lad, have a room in Sherrow's suite. There are several small bedrooms for attendants, pick anyone you like. There is a shared terrace garden where the dog may roam safely." She indicated a door which opened to a snow covered terrace. She took Dudley through a connecting door to the next room.

Morwenna explored the room. There was a sitting area with a fleece rug in front of a large stone fireplace and comfortable cushioned furniture with down pillows covered in shades of blue. A small, finely carved desk and a few bookshelves were against the wall near the fireplace. Windows overlooked a snow-dusted stone terrace.

A doorway led to a second room with a smaller fireplace and a large four-poster bed hung in light blue velvet drapes.

There was also a bathing chamber with a toilet-room and a large bath. She wasn't sure how to fill it, but soon a young Orc maid came to her rooms with a cradle and bedding. Another woman brought soft nappies and pads for the baby and a clay pot with a lid to place the soiled ones inside.

"I am Berta, I will be your personal maid. Would you like me to draw a bath?" She was a tall, big-boned young woman with an upturned nose and bright blue eyes. Her gown was blue, warm and serviceable, with a brown leather laced bodice similar to what Perchka wore.

"Yes. I wasn't sure how to do that."

Berta giggled. "We have a natural hot spring in the mountain, but bath water will need to be mixed with cold water so it is not too hot. I can fill it for you."

Morwenna bathed with her son in the enormous heated pool. Afterward she and Owen played in the sitting room until he was ready for a nap. She joined him in sleep.

Supper was just Sherrow, Dudley, and his mother, held in the small dining room they had eaten in earlier.

"Did you get some rest?" She asked Sherrow.

"Yes, and I will retire shortly after the meal. We will go to my study after we eat. I sent a band of soldiers to capture Baron Krutgar and his men. They will bring them back here. After we get them, I will send messengers to King Alarik. We should have some interesting information for him."

"You will stay here, not go capture them?"

"Yes. My captain is more than capable for this job. Would you like to send men on to your parents' place, to bring them here?"

"Oh, I would love that. But they would not be able to leave their farm."

"I can man a few soldiers there until your parents return. They can take care of the farm."

"Yes, then!"

"After the meal I will have you write them a letter."

They retired to her sitting room soon and Morwenna wrote the letter to her parents.

Dear Mother and Father,

I am writing to you from the Castle Yllamar in northern Hobb. I helped the Queen care for her injured cousin, who is an Orc by bite. Sherrow is the Margrave of Yllamar, an estate of the north and west border of Hobb. We had to flee here due to treachery, but we are safe. My son Owen is with me, growing every day.

Sherrow has extended an invitation for you to join us. He will send men with this letter, who will bring you here if you wish. Some men will stay to care for your farm. The journey will not be too long because Hobb still has Glister magic and can get you here quickly.

Please come! I long to see you and to know you are safe. It looks like war cannot be prevented in Vallanhad, but we will all be safe here.

Your loving daughter,

Morwenna

Sherrow and Dudley sat near the fire, talking about the battle while Own played with his toys. When she was done Sherrow took the letter and gave it to a guard.

"I'm heading to bed. Even with the nap I'm tired," Dudley said. "I'll let Buttercup out on the terrace for a bit." He left for his room, Buttercup trailing behind.

Sherrow sat on the cushioned settee while she got Owen ready for bed. Owen fell asleep soon, and she put him to bed in his cradle.

Sherrow patted the settee, and she sat down beside him.

"Morwenna," Sherrow started to speak but couldn't think of what to say. "You kissed me," he blurted.

"I did. You saved us, Sherrow."

"Yes. Well, I am a good fighter."

Morwenna took his hand in both of hers. "You are a fine man, Sherrow. More than just a fighter. Dudley and Owen just adore you."

"Morwenna... I..." He stopped and frowned. "Marry me Morwenna. I care for you and Owen. I would do my best to keep you safe and happy. I do not like the idea of you being all alone on some estate while war rages."

"Marry you?"

"Yes. I— I care for you Morwenna. You would make a fine wife, and I would do my best to make you happy. I would raise Owen as my heir."

"I care for you, as well. But you are Lord of a castle. Vast holdings. I am a simple farm woman."

Sherrow pulled her close. "But that is best! You will understand the people." He paused. "And that is not the point. I love you and would like to spend our future together."

"You love me?" *Love.* Morwenna cared for Sherrow, had since she had first realized he was not a violent monster, but now she knew her care had turned to love. Tears welled as she thought how blessed she was to have found another love.

"Ah, yes."

Morwenna threw her arms around his neck and pressed her lips to his. "Yes, Sherrow. I love you as well. I want a future with you."

"We will announce the marriage at the feast tomorrow night. Would you like to be married on Yule? Your parents will be here by then."

"I would like that very much."

They cuddled together before the fire until Morwenna gave a huge yawn. They both laughed.

"It has been a very long day. But tomorrow night, why don't we meet here after everyone has gone to sleep?" Sherrow suggested.

"Yes."

Despite her excitement and delight, Morwenna slept very well that night.

WHEN SHE WOKE BERTA was there placing a gown on a stand. "Milady, I have a hot drink for you. Then we will dress you for the day. I found a lovely gown for today and have a green silk gown planned for the feast tonight. You will look perfect!"

"Where did you get the clothing?"

"Perchka filled the Lady's closet with gowns some time ago, anticipating her son would find a bride."

The day dress was soft burgundy wool, with grey fur around the low neckline making it simple to nurse Owen. It fell straight to the floor but was cinched together with a black leather bodice. Underneath she wore a soft chemise and petticoat, plus high woolen stockings. Berta found her a pair of shiny black leather boots that fit well.

Owen, too, had a new wardrobe, bought from a local tailor. She dressed him in bright red tunic with black leggings and small soft boots.

"There. I will remain with you and can change him when necessary, milady. His leather diaper cover is spelled though, so he won't leak."

"Now that is wonderful magic."

Sherrow had already had a cup of her milk earlier, but they all joined for breakfast in the Great Hall, at a table on a Dias, near a huge fireplace.

"Mother," Sherrow said quietly when no servants were nearby. "Morwenna and I have something to tell you."

"Do you now?" Perchka's dark eyes twinkled and she smiled.

"Yes. Tonight I will announce our engagement. We will be married at the midwinter feast."

"Really?" Dudley asked through a mouthful of fried potatoes.

"Yes, but say nothing. I will announce it tonight. Most of our neighbors will come for the feast tonight."

They ate while a dozen people came to be introduced. Later Morwenna toured the castle. She couldn't get enough of the huge kitchen, so warm and fragrant. Every table and counter was busy as food was prepared for the feast. Owen enjoyed the stables and yard, enjoying the company of Buttercup and a number of other palace dogs.

At lunch, she was exhausted. So many people worked here. There we so many different areas, all busy with their work. Owen was getting fussy, so she fed him a bit of table food, then nursed him. "I'm afraid the morning was a bit overwhelming."

"Perhaps you would like to spend the afternoon in your rooms, resting and tending to the little one," Perchka said.

"That would be best." She smiled in relief. "As much as I enjoyed meeting everyone, it is hard to think I will be mistress of all this."

"It will not always be overwhelming, Morwenna," Perchka patted her hand. "Most of the people will be thrilled that you noticed their contribution. They are proud to serve here."

Morwenna took a deep breath, then sipped a chalice of mulled wine. "The staff is wonderful."

"Sherrow also will be taking some rest time in his room."

That was good news. Morwenna was a bit anxious by all the activity Sherrow was doing. Surely he needed more rest? "Good. I was worried he was overdoing all the activity."

"I put him on a healing plan, with rest in the afternoon. No weapon training yet."

Back in her rooms Berta helped her out of her bodice and gown and handed her a warm, soft woolen robe to pull on, and thick fur slippers instead of boots. Owen also received a pair of slippers, which he kept taking off. Finally, though he was ready for an afternoon nap. Morwenna sat on the settee but wondered if she should go to bed.

There was knock at the connecting door, and she flew to it. Sherrow stood there with grin on his face. "Mother wants me to rest until it is time to dress for dinner."

"You can rest with me. Until Owen wakes, anyway. Berta is in her room listening for the baby."

"I think our night will be a long one. There will be dancing and all manner of foolishness."

"Then all the more reason for us to have a little quiet time to ourselves." She drew him to her four-poster bed.

His eyes widened as he stared at the bed, then at her. "We don't have to do anyth—"

Morwenna kissed him, a hard kiss that softened as their lips opened. Her tongue was a sweet fire. He shivered. She finished the kiss by pulling him to bed.

"I am not a shy young girl anymore, Sherrow. I'm a widow with a child. We will be wed soon enough."

"Yes, we will," He managed to gasp out as she untied the simple robe he wore in his rooms. He untied hers, expecting woolen undergarbs but Morwenna was naked, taut pink nipples brushing against his chest, silken long legs, a triangle of reddish brown curls between her legs.

"So beautiful," he murmured, going for another deep passionate kiss while his hands roamed her soft flesh, finding her hard nipples. He trailed his lips down her neck, stunned at how delicate she was, how sweet smelling.

His mouth found her nipple, a faint sweetness of milk there, her breast soft and firm at the same time.

"Mmm, now off with your clothes, so we can be flesh to flesh."

"Yes, milady." Sherrow got out of his clothes and moved to the middle of the bed. He pulled Morwenna on top of him, his hands find new territory as they roved her back and buttocks. "I think you should ride me the first time. Because I can't quite believe this is happening."

She gave a breathy giggle as one long finger found her nub and stroked in tender circles. They kissed, his hands roaming her sweet skin.

"Yes, I will ride you." Her eyes were half closed, lips red and puffy from his kisses. She glided over him and wiggled right on top of his cock before reaching down to guide him.

She slid onto him, wet and tight. Perfect.

"Do you believe it now?"

"Beginning to." His large hands wrapped around her hips, helping her move up and down his shaft for a bit before he moved his finger to her nub once again.

"Ahh, Sherrow." She came around him, inner pulses driving him mad, driving him to ecstasy.

"I think I believe this is real now," he gasped.

Epilogue

YULE NIGHT

The gown was like nothing she'd ever worn before. Heavy cream velvet with white fur at the neckline and sleeves, it fell long and straight to the floor. An embroidered and dyed leather bodice in white and rose went over the gown, laced under her bosom with cords of golden thread. Golden braid, rose-red and green jeweled beads covered the bell sleeves and made a pattern on the skirt. The Orc maid Berta fixed her hair up, in complicated braids and poofs, secured with jeweled pins. White winter roses with ribbons formed a crown.

Owen was dressed to match her. She snorted. "He'll have that filthy in a moment."

"Oh! We have several quilted bibs. We will keep him tidy."

"Are you ready, milady? I will get your father."

Berta brought her father into the room. He looked dapper in black velvet and leather.

"You look like a Queen, my dear." Father offered her his arm, and they followed Berta down the stairs to the Great Hall, which was now filled with people, with only one fireplace blazing. Pine boughs and holly with gold and red ribbons decorated the entire hall and it smelled of pine and exotic spice, mulled cider and fresh bread.

Sherrow waited for her in front of the main fireplace, dressed in dark green velvet, Dudley in black and red at his side. He came to her and took her hand, shaking her father's hand in friendship. Her attendant, dressed in dark rose, was Queen Tadame, who had arrived secretly with the King's Guard summoned to take Baron Krutgar away.

They took their place in front of the fire. Her father joined her mother in the first row of guests, along with another surprise guest, Ann of Amberwood. She had arrived with her twin infants, who were safely asleep in the nursery. Next to her was Ainsley, the page from the caravan. He'd been surprised to learn he had been kidnapped, but please with fostering with Sherrow. He wore new dress boots, courtesy of Morwenna.

A pipe played a long note followed by a slow, haunting melody. Older children dressed in black to represent the night put out the one remaining fire Morwenna and Sherrow stood by. The Hall went dark, the only light was from the stars in the sky that came through the open door to the Great Hall. From the great doorway came six men, older men respected in the community. They pulled a huge log with ropes up through the main aisle and pushed it into the fireplace.

Next came a procession of young women and girls, in their holiday best, each holding a dry stick from the forest. A boy carried a brass basin in which burned a small fire, the last of the old year's log. He walked between the two rows of girls, who lit their stick. As planned they moved to all the fireplaces, and lit the kindling, while the boy stood for Sherrow to light the new log from the remains from the old.

"Witness the light of a new year!" Sherrow called out. "A prosperous year full of good tidings!"

"We see!" The guests cried.

"And now you are all invited to witness my marriage to Lady Morwenna."

Perchka stood forth.

"Do you, Sherrow take my daughter Morwenna as wife forever and for all?"

"I do."

"Do you Morwenna take my son as husband forever and for all?"

"I do."

"By Love, Light and the Glister of Magic, you are now wed," Perchka said, and a cloud of golden glitter surrounded them for a few moments.

"Meet the new Lady of Yllamar, and First Lady of my heart," Sherrow cried.

"Forever and for all!" The crowd shouted, rapping on the tables and floor, making a loud celebration in the night.

The court musicians beat the drums and music filled the Hall while Sherrow and Morwenna shared their first kiss as husband and wife.

The End

Terms and Places of Glister

REALMS OF GLISTER:
Vallanhad
Padawar
Hobb
-Yllamar, Sherrow's northern estate in Hobb
Emrysdell
Hoightlund
Frost Sea
Frostlund
Glister: Sparkling magic once common is the lands
Arcane: Hidden magic, often malevolent

About The Author

BIO

Take a bookworm. Hand her a stack of her much older brother's Sci-fi and fantasy novels, thrillers and horror comics. Then introduce the world of romance.

Make her a jinx. Every great genre TV show she loves gets the ax! So often the romances have no happy ending. She gets upset about no romance in the world and writes her own stories with happy endings.

Throw this all together, shake constantly, and pour onto a computer keyboard.

There!

You have me,

Melisse Aires

Find me!

I have a newsletter! sendfox.com/melisseaires[1]

---

1.   http://sendfox.com/melisseaires

I can always be found on Facebook. I run the fun Scifi Romance Group[2] and also Romancing the Shire[3]. My personal group is Melisse Aires' Lair[4]

BLOG: https://melisseaireswriter.wordpress.com/
Website: http://www.melisseairesbooks.weebly.com[5]
Facebook: https://www.facebook.com/melisseaires
IO News Group:https://groups.io/g/MelisseAiresPureEscapism
Please review if you enjoyed this romance!

---

2.   https://www.facebook.com/groups/the.scifi.romance.group/

3.   https://www.facebook.com/groups/romancingtheshire/

4.   https://www.facebook.com/groups/1732565730395151

5.   http://www.melisseairesbooks.com

Also by Melisse Aires

Another Supernatural Apocalypse
Enchanted Bonds
Ritual of Fire and Ice

A Warm Winter Fantasy
Elf Wish
Christmas Wizardry
Faunication

Cyborg Nation
A Cyborg's Old Terran Christmas

Diaspora Worlds
Her Cyborg Awakes
Alien Blood
Starwoman's Sanctuary

Escaping Poison
Cyborg Security
Diaspora Worlds Bundle
Cyborg Liberation

Encanto Bay--Where Magic Happens
White Tiger Lover
The Psyvamp and the Professor
Holly Jolly Vampire
Single Mom, Vampire Lover

Far Stars Universe
Stranded on Grzbt
Christmas Cookies in Space
Pardblood, A Second Chance Romance

Love on the Space Frontier
Stars Between Us

Realms of Glister
Orc In Winter
Bridal Faire

Urloon
Refugees on Urloon

Standalone
Her Accidental Angel
Warm Winter Fantasies Collection